Licia Oddino

Finn and the Fairies

Illustrated by Alessandra Toni

PURPLE BEAR BOOKS · NEW YORK

IN ARAN VILLAGE people believed in fairies. If a hen stopped laying eggs or a cow went dry or the crops wilted, the villagers were certain the fairies were to blame. So they were careful not to anger the fairies. When they passed through the fairy wood they always bowed politely and said, "By your leave, oh fairies!" And they left bowls of milk—which the fairies loved—outside their doors at night to ward off fairy mischief.

Finn the tailor did *not* believe in fairies. He lived in a small house right next to the fairy wood, but that didn't worry Finn at all. "Fairies!" he would snort. "What foolish superstitions!" He kept to himself, making clothes and tending his beautiful flower garden.

Several miles from Aran Village was the palace of King Bertrand. His son, Prince Nivar, was his pride and joy. When the time came for the prince to marry, the king summoned his chamberlains. "Prince Nivar needs a wife," he declared. "How can we find one for him?"

"You should give a royal ball, Your Majesty," suggested one of the chamberlains.

Invitations written in golden ink were sent to every family in the kingdom, summoning all maidens to the royal ball.

Finn the tailor's skills were known far and wide, and all the maidens wanted him to make their ball gowns. So Finn was soon very busy, sewing gowns in glorious colors, trimmed with the gold of the sun and the silver of the moon.

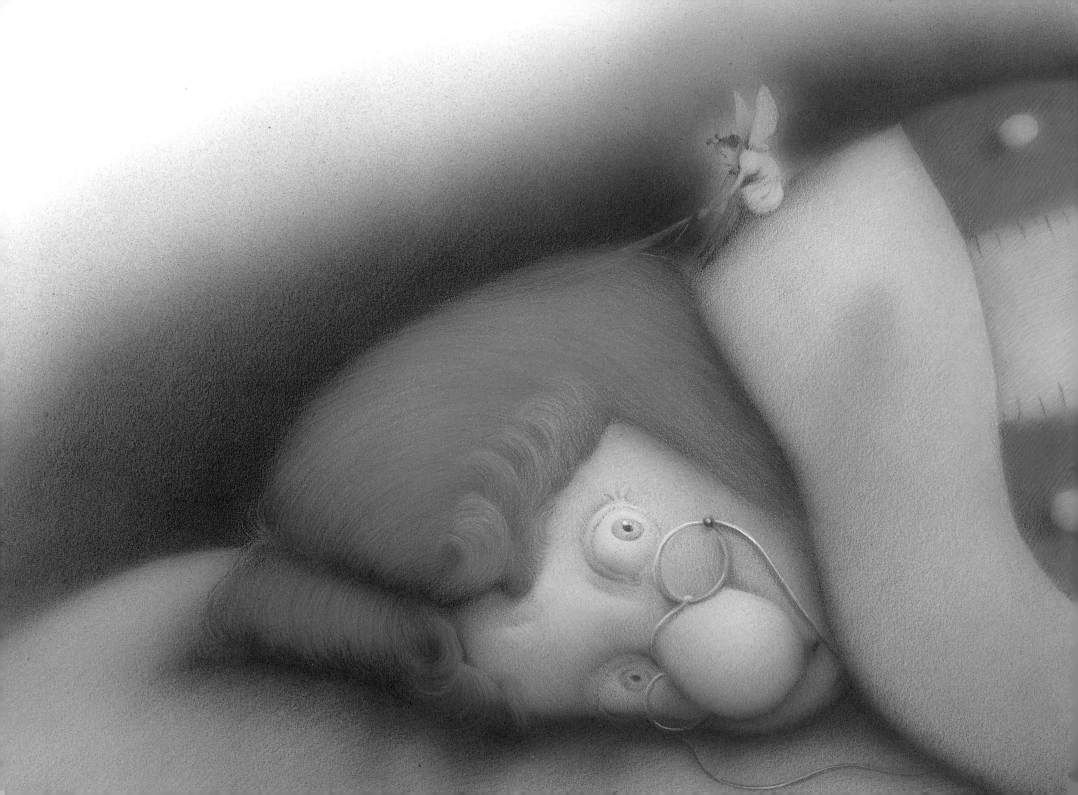

Finn worked night and day. Finally, when he'd finished the very last gown, he fell exhausted into bed. Suddenly he heard a voice right next to his ear.

"Please make us beautiful dresses, too!"

He looked around, but saw no one and so, convinced he had been dreaming, he went back to sleep. But then he felt someone pulling his ear and pinching his nose. And once again he heard the voice. "We want to go to the ball, too."

He turned and saw a tiny creature sitting on his shoulder. Finn could not believe his eyes. There was no doubt at all—this was a fairy! "But I thought fairies weren't real, that they were just a foolish superstition," he stammered, shocked to his toes.

"Oh, we are real, all right, and we want you to make beautiful dresses for us so we can go to the ball, too," said the fairy girl.

"Go away! I am tired. Leave me alone," said Finn and snuggled back under the covers.

The fairy girl had no sooner disappeared than a plate went flying off the shelf, crashing to the floor. Then another, then glasses, bowls, and pots. The bobbins of thread started to unwind and got all tangled together.

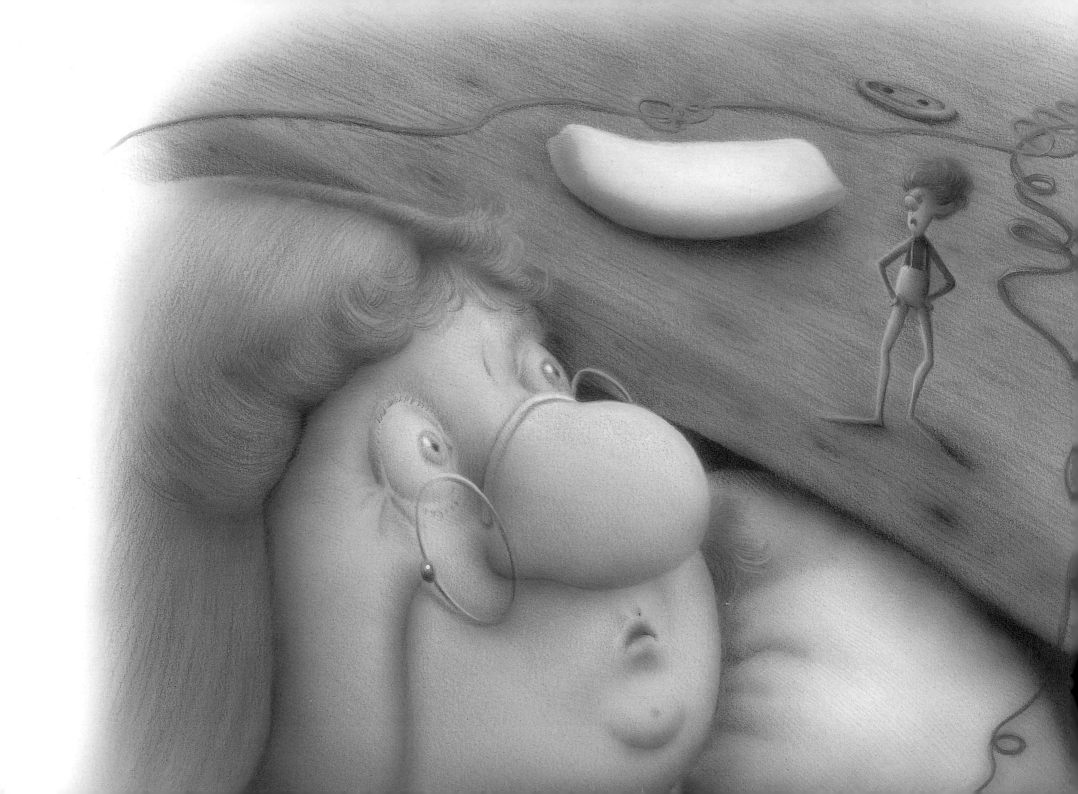

A tiny fairy stood on Finn's worktable, glaring angrily. Sternly, he asked Finn, "Are you going to make the dresses or not?"

A frying pan smashed down on Finn's head. "Enough! Enough! I'll make them!" shouted Finn.

"All right," said the fairy. "We'll be back in the morning."

Finn surveyed the mess in his cottage. This isn't too bad, he thought. Once the maidens pay me for their ball gowns, I'll have plenty of money to fix everything. So why should I bother to make dresses for the fairies? And with that, Finn went back to sleep.

When Finn woke the next morning, he saw the same fairy standing before him.

"Where are the dresses for the fairy girls?" he demanded.

"Uh, uh . . ." stammered Finn.

The fairy looked very angry, and the next thing Finn saw was a pair of scissors fly across the room and start cutting all the beautiful ball gowns into pieces.

Finn's heart sank. He collapsed into his armchair in deep despair.

The fairy asked, "Are you going to make the dresses for the ball?"

"There won't be any royal ball now that the maidens have nothing to wear," moaned Finn. "Oh, woe is me! The king will chop off my head!" And Finn began to cry.

"Listen," said the fairy, taking pity on Finn, "I want to make peace with you. We will help you if you promise to make dresses for us, too."

"The ball is being held to find a wife for Prince Nivar. It is not a ball for you fairies," replied Finn.

The fairy frowned. "Well, then," he said, "we can have our own ball. So is it a deal?"

"We don't have much time!" said Finn.

All of a sudden, a group of fairies appeared. On Finn's directions they flitted around, helping wherever they could. One threaded a needle, another held the cloth while Finn sewed, another handed Finn the buttons. They were all excellent helpers.

The lights in the little cottage remained lit for two nights as Finn and the fairies worked to remake all the ball gowns. One dress was even more lovely than before, for the fairies added a bit of magic dust to it.

They finished just in time.

And on the day of the royal ball, after the maidens had collected their dresses, Finn and the fairies fell asleep at the table, utterly exhausted.

When he woke it was dark, and the fairies were gone. "Oh, dear!" cried Finn. "The fairy ball begins at midnight! I must hurry!"

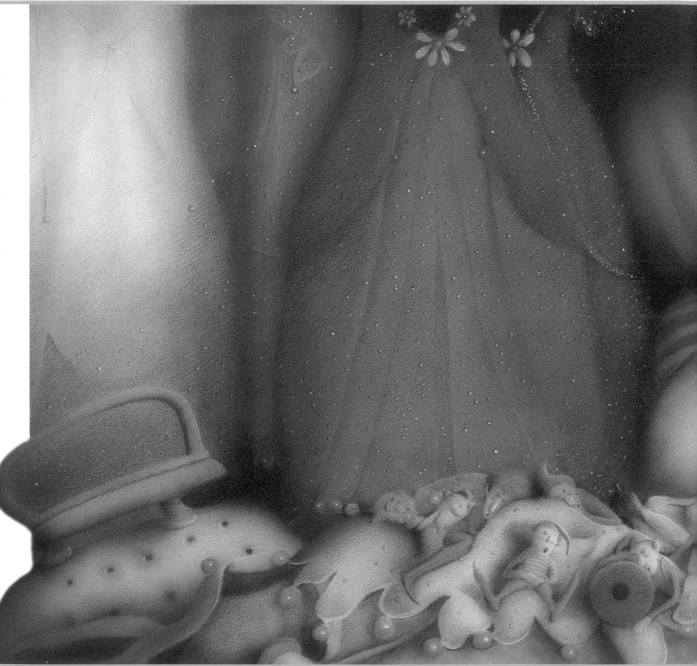

Finn rushed to his shelves in search of material for the fairy dresses, but he had not one single piece left. What could he do?

Just then the moon slid from behind the clouds, shining down on Finn's garden and casting a glow over his beautiful flowers. Finn had an idea. He ran to the garden, gathered a fat bouquet of flowers, and brought it inside.

With great delicacy Finn plucked the flower petals one by one and stitched them to-gether with fine golden thread. His fingers flew, and soon the table was covered with many little dresses in amazing colors.

Finn left the dainty dresses on the table and placed a big bowl of milk beside them. Then he sat down and waited for the fairies.

Meanwhile, at the royal ball, all the young maidens looked lovely, dancing gracefully in their beautiful dresses. Prince Nivar danced all night with one pretty girl who wore the dress sprinkled with fairy dust. Its magic must have worked, for the prince fell madly in love with her. At the end of the ball, the king happily announced their engagement and promised to invite everyone back for a big wedding celebration.

There was another ball that night, the fairy ball, held on a hill beneath the fairy wood. Finn was the only human to be invited.

Finn watched the fairy girls flying around in their beautiful flower dresses. As the moonlight shone on them, they sparkled, and the rich fragrance of the flowers filled the air.

Finn the tailor believes in fairies now. Why, they are his dearest friends!

Library of Congress Cataloging-in-Publication Data is available.

This edition prepared by Cheshire Studio.

TRADE EDITION

ISBN-10: 1-933327-17-0

ISBN-13: 978-1-933327-17-4

10 9 8 7 6 5 4 3 2 1

LIBRARY EDITION

ISBN-10: 1-933327-18-9

ISBN-13: 978-1-933327-18-1

10 9 8 7 6 5 4 3 2 1

Printed in Taiwan